William's Winter Nap

words by Linda Ashman

pictures by Chuck Groenink

𝒟ISNEϷ • HYPERION

Los Angeles   New York

First edition, October 2017
1 3 5 7 9 10 8 6 4 2
FAC-029191-17237
Printed in Malaysia

This book is set in Stempel Schneidler Std/Monotype, Adobe Devanagari/Fontspring
Designed by Phil Caminiti
The illustrations were created in pencils, charcoal, ink, and photoshop

Library of Congress Cataloging-in-Publication Data
Ashman, Linda.
William's winter nap / by Linda Ashman ; illustrated by Chuck Groenink.—First edition.
pages cm
Summary: "A cozy winter bedtime story, featuring a boy and animal characters,
that touches on the concept of hibernation"—Provided by publisher.
ISBN 978-1-4847-2282-4
[1. Stories in rhyme. 2. Bedtime—Fiction. 3. Hibernation—Fiction. 4. Animals—Fiction.] I. Groenink,
Chuck, illustrator. II. Title.
PZ8.3.A775Wi 2017
[E]—dc23   2015008993

Reinforced binding

Visit www.DisneyBooks.com

For Phoebe, Georgia, and Rafe

—L.A.

In a house on a hill
that's tall and steep,
there's a boy named William
who's ready to sleep.

He drinks his cocoa, climbs in bed.
He fluffs the pillow beneath his head,
then burrows down for a nice long nap . . .

but wakes to the sound of a

TAP,

TAP,

TAP.

"Excuse me, but I've lost my way.
I'm cold and tired. May I please stay?"

Will says, "Yes, I'll scooch a bit.
There's room for two—I'm sure we'll fit."

The two climb in and curl up tight.
They YAWN and say,

"*Good night.*"

"Good night."

It's quiet—just the clock's tick tock.

But, wait—what's that? A

KNOCK,

KNOCK,

KNOCK.

"Oh, what a lovely, cozy place!
Could you spare a smidge of space?"

Will says, "Yes, we'll scooch a bit.
There's room for three—I'm sure we'll fit."

The three climb in and curl up tight.
They YAWN and say,

"Good night."

"Good night."

It's peaceful in the sleepy room—
until, that is, the

BOOM! BOOM! BOOM!

"My toes are numb.
My tail is, too.
Okay if I come
in with you?"

Will says, "Yes, we'll scooch a bit.
There's room for four—I'm sure we'll fit."

The four climb in and curl up tight.
They YAWN and say,

"Good night."

"Good night."

PING, PING, PING.
Could that be rain?
No—pebbles on
the windowpane.

"May I come in?
I need some rest.
I promise, I'm
a perfect guest."

Will says, "Yes, we'll scooch a bit.
There's room for five—I'm sure we'll fit."

The five climb in and curl up tight.
They YAWN and say,

"Good night."

"Good night."

The sound of snoring, soft and low,
then—

CRRUNCH!

—some footsteps in the snow.

A note is slipped beneath the door:

"I'd rather not."
"Too squished."
"No space."
"There's got to be some other place."

"We don't have room."
"Too hard to fit."
"No way—
we can't consider it."

Will says, "If it's someone small,
it might not be so hard at all."

He tugs the door to see who's there.

"Uh-oh."

"Oh my."

"What now?"

A . . .

BEAR!

"I saw your light on through the trees.
I'm lonely.
May I join you, please?"

Bear shivers in the falling snow.

"I see. . . .
No room . . .
That's fine. . . .
I'll go."

"It's awfully cold."

"The snow!"
"The ice!"
"He'd keep us warm."
"He seemed quite nice."

They all say, "Wait!
We'll scooch a bit.
There's room for six—
somehow we'll fit."

The six climb in and curl up tight.
They YAWN and say,

"*Good night.*"

"*Good night.*"

"Sweet dreams, my friends,"
says Will. "Sleep tight.
I'll see you in the warm spring light."